Ignatius Finds Help

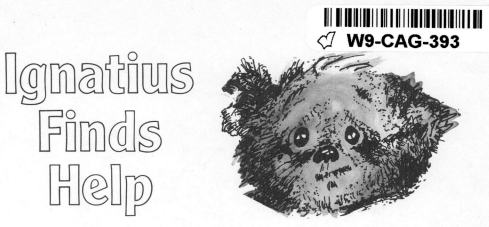

A Story About Psychotherapy For Children

Written by
Matthew Galvin, M.D.

Illustrated by
Sandra Ferraro

Magination Press
A Division of Brunner/Mazel Publishers
New York

Library of Congress Cataloging-in-Publication Data

Galvin, Matthew.
    Ignatius finds help.

    Summary: Ignatius, a bear who has trouble getting
along with others at home and school, visits a
psychotherapist, Dr. Pelican, whose innovative
techniques help Ignatius to solve his problems.
    [1. Psychotherapy—Fiction.   2. Bears—Fiction]
I. Ferraro, Sandra, ill.   II. Title.
PZ7.G1423Ig   1988   [Fic]   87-34899
ISBN 0-945354-01-0
ISBN 0-945354-00-2 (soft)

Copyright © 1987 by the Child Psychiatry Section,
Department of Psychiatry, Indiana University

First Magination Press Edition 1988

Published by
Magination Press
A Division of Brunner/Mazel, Inc., 19 Union Square West, New York, NY 10003

Distributed in Canada by
Book Center
1140 Beaulac St., Montreal, Quebec H4R 1R8, Canada

MANUFACTURED IN THE UNITED STATES OF AMERICA

10 9 8 7 6 5 4 3

TO OUR FAMILIES

ACKNOWLEDGMENTS

The author expresses thanks to James E. Simmons, M.D., Takuya Sato, M.D., and the late Nancy Roeske, M.D., for their valuable criticisms about the story's content and to the teachers at Larue Carter School for their suggestions on improving the story's form. The author expresses special thanks to Dottie Maguire who prepared the manuscript.

The illustrator thanks her family, Bart, Cassidy and Ty, for their support and interest in her endeavors as an artist.

FOREWORD TO PARENTS

One morning I accompanied my young son to the dentist's office. While we waited, he picked up a book and asked me to read it to him. The story we read together had to do with a child's first visit to the dentist. I reflected that there were no books in the waiting room of our child psychiatry unit having to do with a family's first visit to a child psychotherapist. We did provide families with fact sheets about different kinds of emotional, mental and behavioral disorders but these did not seem to hold a child's interest.

This storybook is intended to be read by the child with and without his/her parents. It is not a storybook for any child but rather the child who has been referred with his/her parents for psychotherapy. It is meant to assist the child in having realistic expectations about what might happen in the course of evaluation and treatment. Hopefully, this story may also assist the child and family in talking together about their first visit to a psychotherapist. It is not intended to be read as a statement about how psychotherapy should be conducted for your family and your child.

Ignatius sat sadly in his cubby-hole in the den. He didn't cry. He was much too tough a little bear to cry. "It isn't fair!" Ignatius thought to himself. "That nasty raccoon started it!" He rubbed the side of his nose. It had just begun to swell up. It was hard to breathe. "He started it . . . and I finished it," he said. He was pretty pleased with himself after all.

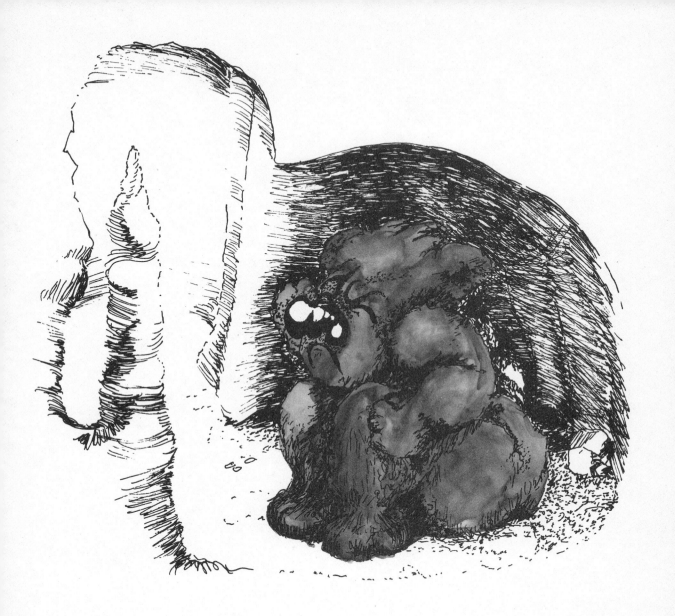

Mommy Bear and Daddy Bear were arguing in another part of the den. Mommy Bear was saying that Ignatius had been in too many fights since school had started. "He's too rough with the other animals in school. That's what his teacher says. He doesn't know how to play nicely." She was doing what she called her Dancing Bear work-out while she talked.

Daddy Bear sighed and said, "Well, he's a bear, isn't he?" He told her, "There are some pretty tough customers in the forest. A bear really needs to know how to defend himself."

Mommy Bear gave him one of her long Bear-glares. She said Ignatius was too rough with her too. "And he squeezes the cub until her eyes bulge out. He's too . . . too hugnacious."

There was a new addition to the family: little sister cub. Ignatius had just learned about addition in school, and he didn't like it one bit. He especially did not like the new addition at home. He simply couldn't believe how much fuss everyone made over her. But there were times she smiled at him or made a silly face. Then, he felt a warm feeling inside him creeping up to his ears and down to his paws. When that happened, he wanted to hold her. Mommy Bear would put her in his lap with pillows all around. She would smile and say, "Now be gentle."

Other times, Mommy Bear was busy getting ready to nurse. Then, she would try to shoo him away. So Ignatius would grab his sister for a quick hug or pinch her on the cheek. She would cry. Mommy Bear would say, "Gracious, Ignatius. You're too hugnacious." Ignatius would sulk and whine and make things worse until Mommy Bear swatted his behind.

Ignatius was getting drowsy even though his nose was aching and throbbing. He had just begun to sleep when he heard the crash in the kitchen.

Daddy Bear was loud and snarly. Ignatius heard a few words like "overtime" and "swingshift." He knew those words. They meant Daddy Bear and he would not be going to the wrestling match Saturday night. They wouldn't go trout fishing Sunday morning either. He had heard the words a lot since Daddy Bear started working at the mead factory. Now Mommy Bear was mad too. She wanted some time of her own. She wanted more help around the den. The door slammed. Ignatius knew Daddy Bear had gone.

Ignatius fell asleep. He dreamt he lived alone in a great hollow
tree. When he wanted to, he could climb to the very top of the tree
and peer down at the forest below. No one could reach him in his
tree. He felt safe. Sometimes, though, from his high perch, he
would hear laughter in the distance. He could make out the
shapes of young animals of all sorts playing together. They saw
him in his tree and began to tease him: "Goodness gracious,
Ignatius is too hugnacious."

He felt lonely and angry.
He threw twigs and pieces
of bark down at them
until they scattered.
Ignatius looked up at the
sky and saw more
emptiness than stars.

The next morning, Mommy Bear took Ignatius to see the family doctor because he couldn't breathe through his nose. The family doctor looked at Ignatius' nose and ordered an x-ray, but he seemed more interested in how Ignatius was getting along at home and school. He told Ignatius and his mother not to worry about the nose, which would get better. Then he said he was worried about all the problems Ignatius was having at home and at school. The family doctor said he would like for Ignatius and his mother to see Dr. Pelican. "Who's Dr. Pelican?" Ignatius asked.

"Dr. Pelican is a doctor who listens and talks to young bears with problems like yours," the family doctor answered: "He's called a psychotherapist."

Mommy Bear made an appointment for Ignatius and her to see Dr. Pelican. Before the first visit Ignatius was worried. He wondered what kind of talking and listening Dr. Pelican would do. He wondered if it would hurt very much.

The day came when Ignatius and Mommy Bear went to see Dr. Pelican. Ignatius decided not to fuss about it. In fact, he was a little bit curious. Dr. Pelican met them outside his office. He invited them in. Dr. Pelican wanted to know what was happening at home and school. Ignatius told Dr. Pelican a little. Then Mommy Bear told Dr. Pelican a lot more than Ignatius liked. Even so, Ignatius found out that seeing Dr. Pelican wasn't scary at all. Ignatius was surprised when Dr. Pelican said the visit was almost over. The time had passed very quickly.

Dr. Pelican said that next time he would see Ignatius by himself. They would talk more and maybe visit the playroom. Not only that, Dr. Pelican wanted to see Ignatius' father. Hearing that, Mommy Bear burst into tears. She said she didn't know whether Daddy Bear would see Dr. Pelican or not. She explained about the big fight and how Daddy Bear had walked out in a terrible huff.

Ignatius suddenly became very redfaced. In an angry voice he said, "He's not my real father." Now, Ignatius could barely remember his real father who had gone away a long time ago — when Ignatius was just a cub. And, really, if he hadn't been so angry just then, he might have admitted that Daddy Bear did a lot of things with him that fathers do with their cubs.

Mommy Bear cried, but she promised she would talk with Daddy Bear about going to see Dr. Pelican with her and Ignatius. Dr. Pelican also told Ignatius that he would call Ms. Puma, the school teacher. Ignatius didn't see how that would help, but he said "O.K." anyway.

Ignatius and his mother came back to see Dr. Pelican every week. Daddy Bear had returned to the den, but he refused to see Dr. Pelican. If you had asked Ignatius whether anything had changed at home or school, he would have told you "No — not a thing." Even so, he did notice that his mother was letting him know when he had been a good cub and when he had been bad. He also noticed that he was getting some special help for addition.

Sometimes he would see Dr. Pelican alone, and they would tell stories to one another. Ignatius made up a story about a little bear who felt his parents didn't want him at home. The little bear ran away to live by himself. He found a high, hollow tree in the forest and climbed to the very top. In his tree he felt safe and secure but also a bit lonely. In the story, the little bear heard laughter and playing down below. Then he saw a group of cubs running and chasing one another and looking for honey. He climbed down from the tree to join them. They let him look for honey with them.

But when they found some, there was a quarrel because Ignatius ate most of the honey. He simply would not share. The other bears ran away and left him alone. After that the honey didn't taste very good.

Then Dr. Pelican told his own stories. They started out pretty much like Ignatius' stories did, but he ended them differently. In one story, Dr. Pelican told about the little bear who wouldn't share his honey because there wasn't enough to go around. The little bear liked his honey a lot, but it made him thirsty. He looked and looked for something to drink. As hard as he looked he couldn't find anything — not even water. He became more and more thirsty as he ate his honey. Then he saw someone coming down the forest path. It was Maggie-the-Calf carrying a pail of milk her mother had given her. The little bear was so thirsty that he asked Maggie to give him some milk. She said there wasn't enough to go around, and she intended to drink it all up.

Dr. Pelican asked Ignatius to finish the story. Ignatius thought for a while. At first he thought the little bear should just take the milk and run away as fast as he could. But somehow he didn't like that ending. He thought some more. Finally, he decided that the little bear could offer Maggie some honey in exchange for the milk. That way they both could have a little honey and a little milk. They would share.

That night Ignatius had another dream. He dreamt he was in the great hollow tree, high above the forest. The night was still and warm. But he didn't feel right. He was restless and couldn't get comfortable. Then he had a thought, well, almost a thought. It was more like a quiet, friendly whisper inside him. It seemed to say, "Come down out of your tree, Ignatius . . . Come down out of your tree."

When Ignatius awakened the next morning, he went for a walk in the forest. He really hoped he would meet somebody new who hadn't heard about his hugnacious ways and who just might want to be his friend. He became aware of a rustling sound off the path. He stopped and listened. He walked a little farther. He heard the sound again. Suddenly he caught sight of a bushy tail. He decided that whoever it was hadn't noticed him. He would circle back and catch it by surprise. Keeping close to the ground, he crept up to the gooseberry bush. The stranger in the bush made it shake this way and that.

Ignatius leapt, his paws held wide open to give the stranger a great big surprise hug. Too late Ignatius saw the white stripes that told him the stranger was a skunk!

Holding her nose, Mommy Bear soaked Ignatius with tomato juice to get rid of the odor. She shook her head and said, "It serves you right for being too hugnacious." At first Ignatius thought that making friends just wasn't worth the effort, but he decided to talk about what had happened with Dr. Pelican. Well, Ignatius tried to talk about the problem but he couldn't! The words wouldn't come out. He was too frustrated and upset.

Dr. Pelican listened a while and then stopped Ignatius. Ignatius expected another story; but, instead, Dr. Pelican said he had an idea. He was going to call Ms. Puma. He would ask her to send some addition problems for Ignatius to do in the doctor's office. Ignatius couldn't believe it: now he would have to do addition instead of tell stories!

That evening, Ignatius looked across the table at Daddy Bear who was already on his third cup of mead. Ignatius told him about his visit to Dr. Pelican. Daddy Bear exclaimed, "Addition? He doesn't get paid to teach you addition! Your Dr. Pelican is a very strange bird."

"I wonder what he's up to," Daddy Bear grumbled as he stumbled out the door.

The next time he visited Dr. Pelican, Ignatius carried along some addition problems from Ms. Puma's class. Dr. Pelican asked to see them. Then, the doctor began talking to himself. Ignatius had a wild hope that Dr. Pelican would do all his homework for him. The hope quickly faded. Dr. Pelican wanted him to do some problems right then and there.

"But I can't," cried Ignatius, "I don't know how." And he threw his homework on the floor: "I'm too dumb!"

Dr. Pelican picked up the homework. He said sometimes he
had trouble with homework too. "That's why I talk to
myself," he added with a smile. Ignatius listened to what
Dr. Pelican said to himself when he was working a problem.
He started by saying, "Hmm. What am I supposed to do
here?" Then he would answer himself by saying something
like, "Oh I see . . . I'm supposed to add 12 and 17. The sign
tells me what to do." Then he would copy the numbers on
his paper. "I wonder what the answer is?" he said. "I guess I
have to think hard and just try to solve the problem. There
isn't a list of answers here."

"Nope." said Ignatius, "It's in the back of the book." Ignatius tried to turn the pages to the back.

Dr. Pelican said, "No, no. I think I can do it if I just think hard." He wrote down an answer. "Now," Dr. Pelican said, "see if I'm right." Ignatius looked, and sure enough Dr. Pelican was right. Dr. Pelican said, "I did a good job." Ignatius had to agree. "You try the next problem, Ignatius," said Dr. Pelican, "and be sure to talk yourself through." Ignatius did talk himself through the problem, but he didn't say he had a done a good job. Dr. Pelican told him to tell himself he had done well.

At the end of the visit Ignatius and Dr. Pelican left the office together. Dr. Pelican remembered he had forgotten his black bag, but he had closed the door. Now, the door was the kind that locked by itself when it was closed. Dr. Pelican couldn't open it because the keys were in his black bag. "That really ruffles my feathers," said Dr. Pelican. Ignatius could tell he was flustered. Then he seemed to calm down as he thought about the problem.

Dr. Pelican said, "Hmm. What am I supposed to do about this?" He thought a while. "Well, I have a spare key at home — I could go get it and bring it back."

Ignatius thought, "You could bust open the door or break a window to get in."

Dr. Pelican thought some more, "I could call a locksmith." Dr. Pelican said, "I think I'll just go home. I probably won't need my bag tonight. I'll just bring the spare key tomorrow. Leaving my key in the black bag was a mistake. I'll have to think of someplace better to put it."

"You did a good job,"
Ignatius said and laughed.
Dr. Pelican laughed too.

Ignatius was a little excited about what he had learned. In school, Ms. Puma let him practice his problem-solving skills. She told him not to talk to himself too loud. His classmates thought it was funny that he whispered to himself. But some of them asked what he was doing. "Problem-solving," said Ignatius. Ms. Puma explained problem-solving to the class. Ignatius whispered to himself more and more softly. Finally, no one could hear him except himself.

One day, Ignatius brought his homework to show his parents.
"How did you do so well?" said Daddy Bear.

"Problem-solving," said Ignatius. "Dr. Pelican taught me how."

Daddy Bear said that he should pay a visit to "that strange bird."
Mommy Bear said "I think we could go with Ignatius next week.
Can you take off work?"

Daddy Bear grumbled, "That will
mean using another sick-day."
He looked at Mommy Bear,
"Well, we'll see."

Time passed. Ignatius thought it was fine and dandy that he did better in Ms. Puma's class. Daddy Bear and Mommy Bear were seeing Dr. Pelican by themselves for a while. Dr. Pelican still saw Ignatius by himself, but not as often. "Still," Ignatius thought to himself, "I don't have any friends." He remembered the meeting with the skunk and sighed.

Dr. Pelican told Ignatius he looked sad. Dr. Pelican asked why. Ignatius said everything was fine. Dr. Pelican asked about home and school. Ignatius said everything was fine. But Ignatius didn't tell him about the fight he had with Penelope Porcupine. Just then, Ignatius started to cry. "Nobody likes me because I'm too hugnacious."

Dr. Pelican patted him softly on the shoulder. He said, "Ignatius, I thought bears were just naturally hugnacious." Dr. Pelican had that problem-solving look again, "Hmm. Let's see."

"The problem is you want to make friends. You want to be liked, right?" Ignatius nodded. Dr. Pelican went on, "And you try to make friends hugnaciously, right?" Ignatius nodded again.

"Well, you know, Ignatius, I see lots of different animals from the forest. Some animals like a good hug now and then — but not all the time and not from just anybody. Some animals don't like hugs at all. Hugs make them feel too closed in, I guess. But most animals do like to know somehow, someway, when you like them." Dr. Pelican asked, "What do you think?"

Ignatius thought about what Dr. Pelican had said. Then, he answered, "I think maybe the problem is this: I need to find out how to show different animals that I like them and want to be friends."

"Right," said Dr. Pelican. "Now we have to think of different ways to solve the problem."

Ignatius had to work on the problem
a very long time. He watched other
animals making friends. He asked
them, "How can I show you that I
like you?" He learned that Ryan
Raccoon liked a bit of a scratch
behind the ears.

Penelope Porcupine liked to
almost touch noses before
she scurried away.

Bartholomew the Otter didn't like to be touched, but he sure did enjoy a good swim.

Some animals liked to hear "Good morning. How are you?" Some animals liked to just sit quietly.

Now, Ignatius noticed that sometimes he felt like hugging even when he knew that the other animals didn't want to be hugged. Worse than that, Ignatius noticed that sometimes when he wanted to hug — it wasn't always because he wanted to show the animals he liked them! He talked this over with Dr. Pelican. Dr. Pelican asked if Ignatius could be hugnacious in ways that wouldn't hurt anybody. He thought it would be good if the whole family could talk this problem over with him.

Sure enough, Daddy and Mommy Bear had some ideas. Daddy Bear thought it was a good idea for Ignatius to join the school wrestling team. Mommy Bear said, "O.K. if you keep your grades up." Ignatius was delighted. He really wanted to wrestle. Daddy Bear promised to teach him some holds.

All of the bears talked with each other and Dr. Pelican about different ways to show different feelings. And, as time went on, Ignatius learned to hug without being too hugnacious. He learned to solve all kinds of problems. He also learned to wrestle by the rules.

Still, sometimes when he hugged
his little sister, I have to admit,
he hugged just a bit too hard.